Plop!
Secrets of Poo Power

Written by
John Townsend

Next time you switch on a light, think again …

Do you know what can make a light bulb work?

Here is a clue. It has four legs and it gives us milk.

(It may even have two legs and be closer to home! But more of that later.)

Yes, a cow.

Cows give us much more than milk. They make poo – lots of it!

Cow **dung** can be useful. When it rots down and dries, it can make gas. This is called **biogas**.

Biogas is made here

Biogas burns well. We can burn this gas to make **electricity**.

Gas from poo can help keep your TV on.
The amount of poo that a cow produces in one day can power two light bulbs for 24 hours.
Gas from 500 cows can power 100 homes. That's super poop!

Dog poo can make gas too. A park in the USA turns dog poo into light.

When dog owners walk their dogs in the park, they 'scoop the poop'. Then they put the poo in a 'Park Spark' tank.

Gas is made inside the tank – and it powers street lights.

Now for a big surprise …

Your poo can also make biogas. A few towns now turn human poo into gas.

It makes sense: there are many more humans than cows on our planet. We could make a lot of electricity from so much poo.

One day we may heat and light all our homes using 'toilet power'.

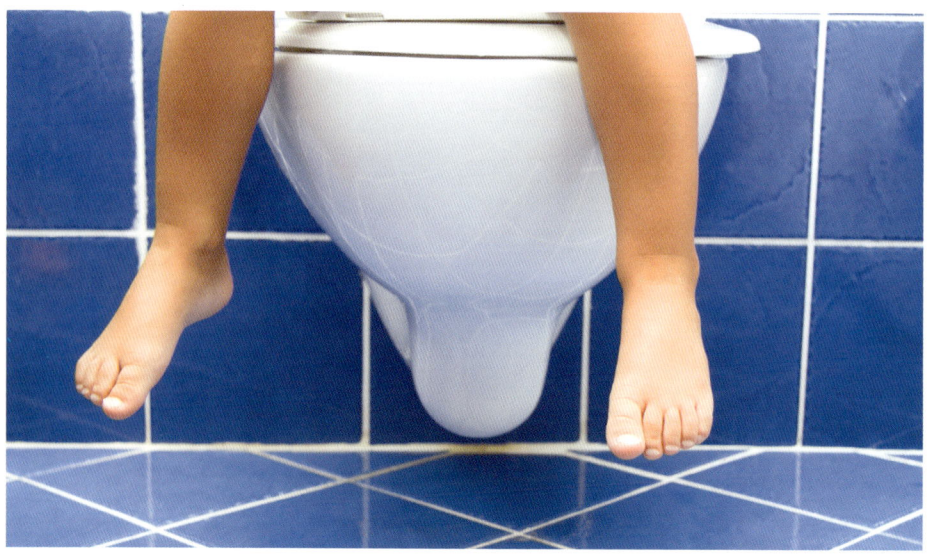

In a year you make about 30kg of poo (when it is dried). That weighs the same as about 30 bags of sugar.

In a lifetime you poo about 15 tonnes. That weighs about the same as three elephants!

So where does it all go?

When you flush a toilet, the poo moves along **sewer pipes**.

These lead to big tanks at a **sewage treatment centre**.

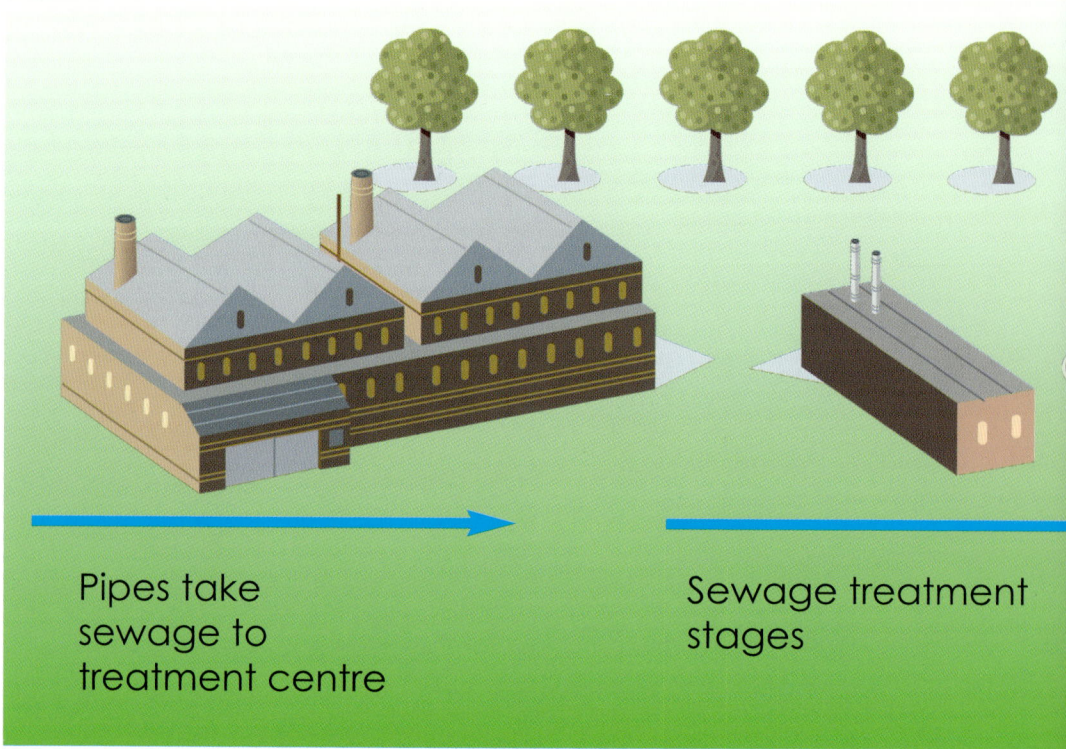

Pipes take sewage to treatment centre

Sewage treatment stages

The sewage treatment centre makes clean water from dirty waste.

The poo soon sinks and rots down. After a while, the **sludge** that is left can be used to make biogas.

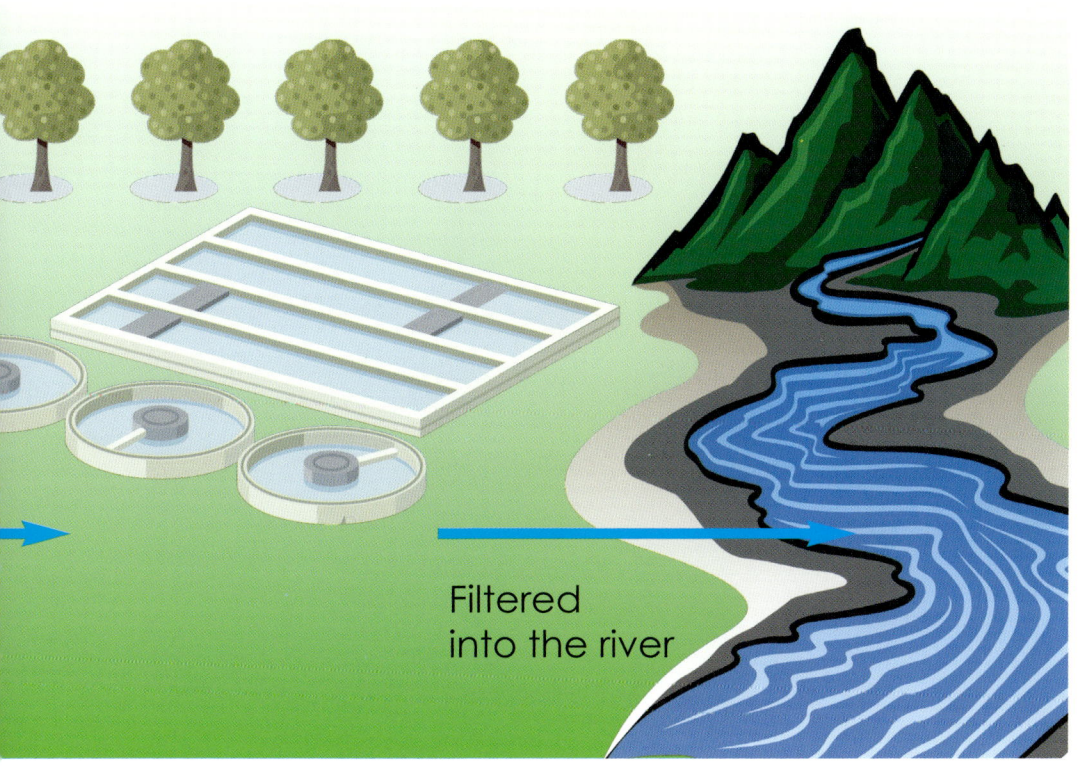

Filtered into the river

Can you believe it?

A company in Japan has made a motorbike that runs on human biogas.

The bike doesn't really have a toilet for the driver!

It has a seat that *looks like* a toilet, just to show everybody its engine runs on biogas.

Most cars run on **petrol**.

Petrol is made from oil that has to be pumped up from rocks.

One day the oil will run out.

So can we ever run cars on biogas?

The answer is simple – YES! In fact, one day we may have to.

Some cars already run on biogas. Toilets can keep them full of fuel!

This Bio-Bug runs on biogas from human poo. The VW 'dung beetle' can go 10,000 miles a year. That's using the toilet waste from just 70 houses.

If cars can run on poo, what about buses?
Again, the answer is – YES!
Some buses already run on biogas.

The UK's first 'poo bus' ran from Bristol and Bath in 2014. This 40-seater 'Bio-Bus' runs on gas from sewage and food waste.

A single tank of gas comes from five people's waste in a year. That keeps the bus going for 190 miles (305km).

All aboard the number two!

Gas from poo is called **'green energy'**. That means it's better for our planet than burning coal or oil.

After all, poo will never run out. It will always be with us.

Our bottoms can save the Earth!

Index

bio-bike   *10*
Bio-Bug   *12*
bio-bus   *14*
biogas   *3, 6, 11, 12*
cow dung   *3*
electricity   *3*
green energy   *15*
'Park Spark' tank   *5*
petrol   *11*
sewer pipes   *8*
sewage treatment centre   *8*
sludge   *9*